This edition published by Parragon Books Ltd in 2017
and distributed by

Parragon Inc.
440 Park Avenue South, 13th Floor
New York, NY 10016
www.parragon.com

ISBN 978-1-4748-6868-6

Printed in China

SCOOBY-DOO!™

Bath · New York · Cologne · Melbourne · Delhi
Hong Kong · Shenzhen · Singapore

It was a big day for the Mystery, Inc. gang. They were on their way to get some of their treasures valued on the Antique Attic Show.

"These items are sure to be worth a fortune," Fred said.

"Hey, look what Scooby's found!" Shaggy cried.

Velma looked at Scooby's discovery. "It looks like a skeleton key."

"Wow! A skeleton key is supposed to open anything! We can find out more once we get to the show," said Fred. "Let's go!"

"Ruh-roh," Scooby said when they arrived. The mansion where the Antique Attic Show was held looked old and dark.

"Zoinks!" Shaggy added. "This place is creepy!"

"You can say that again," Velma said.

"I'm Mr. Biggy," said a man in a suit, standing by the entrance. "Go right in. We've been expecting you."

The gang stepped inside, and the door closed behind them.

Inside, people waited in lines to have their treasures valued. Daphne hurried to the booth that specialized in teddy bears. Velma showed her cuckoo clock to the clock expert. Fred couldn't find a booth for old lamps, so he went to the "Worthless Junk" line.

The gang was so busy with their treasures that none of them noticed a very interesting pattern on one of the walls. . . .

Keyzax the wizard was busy looking at the key in Shaggy's hand.
"There's something fishy about this guy, Scoob," Shaggy whispered.

"Rish? Rhere?" Scooby asked. He sniffed the air.

"Not fish," Shaggy said. "Fishy. This guy is up to something."

Just then, Keyzax thrust his hand forward and grabbed the key.

"I knew something fishy was going on here!" Shaggy cried.

"Help!" Shaggy shouted as he and Keyzax fought over the key.

"Grrrrrrr!" Scooby held on to the wizard's cape with his teeth.

While Scooby wrestled with Keyzax, a hand pushed aside the red curtain. A tall, thin man in a dark suit stood behind it, watching them.

The wizard finally tore away from Scooby and tried to make his escape.

Just then, the lights began to flicker. Everyone ran for the door. "Look out! It's the ghost of Admiral Blightey!" Keyzax shouted.

The gang turned to see an eerie form standing in the middle of the crowd. It wore an eyepatch and a sea captain's uniform. The high-pitched sound of a whistle pierced the air.

Then Velma spotted the hand grasping the curtain. "I think I'm beginning to understand what a skeleton crew is!" she said.

Suddenly, the lights went out and the ghost disappeared!

"Hang on to that key, Scooby," Velma said. "Something's going on here, and I want to know what!"

"Quick, turn on your flashlights," Fred commanded. "It's time to split up and solve this mystery. Shaggy, you and Scooby search downstairs, and we'll go upstairs. Keep your eyes peeled for clues."

Fred, Velma, and Daphne crept up the stairs and came to a door.
"Check out all this old stuff!" Fred said. The walls were covered
with muskets, swords, medals, ribbons, and more.

"Look!" Fred cried. "The ghost must have dropped his whistle."
He'd spied an old sea captain's whistle by Velma's feet.

"Wait a minute, Fred," Velma said. "There's something about
this whistle that isn't too ghostly."

"Come on, gang," Fred said. "We must leave no door unopened! There are sure to be more clues." He opened the door to a room filled with old ship wheels, cannons, and flags. And that wasn't all.

"Look at that!" Velma said, pointing to a treasure chest in the middle of the room. A plaque on the chest read "Admiral Blightey's Treasure."

"Jeepers!" Daphne cried.

"Jeepers is right, Daphne!" Fred said. "Let's get a closer look at that chest."

But trouble was waiting for the gang. Suddenly, the floor in front of the chest opened up beneath them.

"Whoaaaaa! A trapdoor!" Fred yelled as they all fell through.

"This ghost-hunting is making me hungry, Scoob," Shaggy said as they searched for clues. "Let's find the kitchen."

Scooby and Shaggy crept along the hallway in silence until . . .

"Arrrrrrrr!"

"Like, the ghost'll hear your stomach growling, Scooby!" Shaggy said.

"Rit rasn't re. Rit ras rim," Scooby replied, pointing behind them.

"Zoinks!" Shaggy cried. "Run, Scooby! It's the ghost!"

Scooby and Shaggy took cover in a dark closet. They slammed the door, shutting out the ghost.

"Hee hee hee! That tickles, Scoob!" Shaggy whispered.

"Rit rasn't re!" Scooby cried. "Rit ras rim."

They were shocked to see Admiral Blightey waiting to trap them!

"Zoinks!" Shaggy yelled again. "Like, how'd he get in here?"

Meanwhile, Fred, Daphne, and Velma found themselves standing in another room of the mysterious mansion—and they were locked in! Velma was busy looking at the trapdoor they had just fallen through. "Hey, gang, look at this groovy hat I found," Daphne said.

Fred had spotted something even better. "Very interesting," he said. "Come here and check out these keys. They look exactly like the one Scooby found!"

Scooby and Shaggy were busy running away from Admiral Blightey.
"Like, head for that hole in the wall, Scoob!" Shaggy said.

The BOOM! BOOM! BOOM! of the ghost's heavy footsteps close
behind made them run even faster.

Shaggy was running so fast that he didn't notice a clue on the shoe
that was so close to him. . . .

Shaggy and Scooby slammed smack into a heavy wooden door.
"Zoinks!" Shaggy screamed. "We're trapped!"

The ghost moved toward Shaggy and Scooby. He almost had them!

Shaggy and Scooby hammered on the door, and accidentally pushed
a button. In the nick of time, the floor opened up under Admiral Blightey!
"Arrrrrrrr!" yelled the ghost as he fell through another trapdoor.

Back in the locked room,
the doorknob started to twist and turn.

"The ghost!" Fred, Velma, and Daphne screamed.

Just then, the door burst open . . . to reveal Shaggy and Scooby!

Shaggy was scared. "Like, that ghost is everywhere at once! We hid
from it in a closet, but it was already there, waiting for us!" he cried.

"Huddle up, gang," Fred said. "I've got a plan." He whispered to
them, and then said out loud, "We'll head up to the treasure room."

The whole gang was in place in the treasure room, ready for Fred's big plan. The skeleton key was on the floor in front of the chest, close to the edge of the trapdoor.

"Get ready, gang!" Fred whispered. "Here comes the ghost!"

The gang watched silently as Admiral Blightey reached for the key. Fred pulled a piece of string, slowly moving the key along the floor.

When the ghost had both feet on the trapdoor, Shaggy pulled down on the candlestick.

"Arrrrrr!" The trapdoor opened and the ghost fell through!

"Jeepers!" Daphne yelped. "We got the ghost!"

"Zoinks!" Shaggy cried. "Here comes another one!"

"Arrrrrr!" the second ghost cried, falling through the trapdoor.

"Don't move, gang, there's one more on the way," Fred said.

Then they saw the thin man in the dark suit creep in and move toward the key. He reached for it, but lost his balance. With a clatter, he tumbled through the trapdoor, too!

Downstairs, two police officers were waiting to arrest the three villains as they fell into their own trap.

"Two ghosts. That's how the ghost could be in two places at once," Fred said. "Now, let's unmask them."

"Zoinks, that's Mr. Biggy!" Shaggy said.

"And Keyzax the wizard!"

"Good work, kids," one of the police officers said. "These criminals stole that treasure chest from a museum ten years ago."

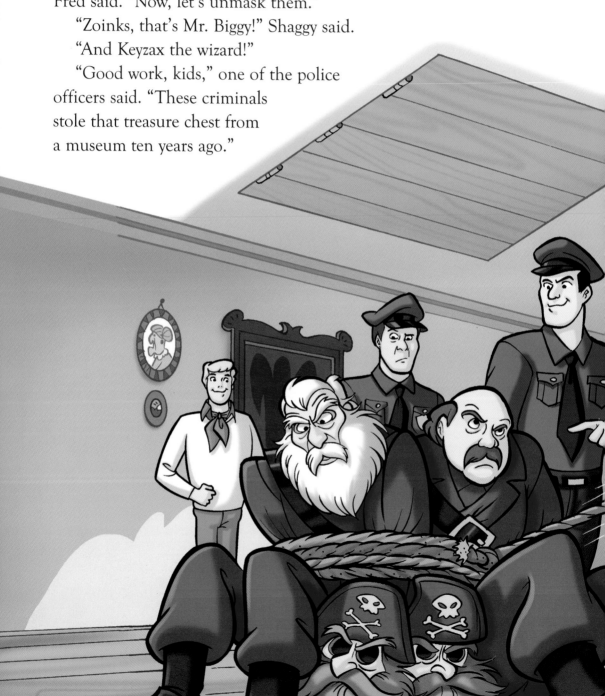

"Admiral Blightey buried the key somewhere else for safekeeping. We've been looking for it ever since, using this Antique Attic Show," the thin man said.

"Zoinks, Scoob, and you found it!" Shaggy said.

"Please let me just see the treasure chest opened before you take me away," the thin man begged.

"Ruh-roh," Scooby said, when he realized the key was lost again.

The gang quickly retraced their steps and luckily they soon found the key hanging from the trapdoor.

"Phew!" they all sighed with relief.

Then everyone headed up to the treasure room, excited to reveal the last element of the mystery.

"Here goes," Velma said. They all held their breath as she turned the key and the treasure chest opened. . . .

Sparkling jewels, shiny doubloons, and treasures beyond their wildest dreams overflowed from inside the chest.

"That's some treasure," Fred sighed. "And now it can go back to the museum for everyone to see."

"Like, I don't know," Shaggy said. "The only treasure I want to see right now is a box of Scooby Snacks!"

"Ree, roo!" Scooby agreed. "Scooby-dooby-doo!"